To my sweet Simon. Dream big!
—J.R.

For Jeff—thank you for showing me
the fantastic stories in the book about you.
—J.C.

ISBN 978-0-06-304150-9

The artist used Photoshop to create the illustrations for this book.
Typography by Amy Ryan
21 22 23 24 25 PC 10 9 8 7 6 5 4 3 2 1
❖
First Edition

WHAT WOULD YOU DO IN A BOOK ABOUT YOU?

By Jean Reidy

Pictures by Joey Chou

HARPER
An Imprint of HarperCollinsPublishers

HOOOOOOOO!

Who?
What about you?
Me?
You!

What would you do?

The story starts now.
Your tale is brand-new.

What would you do in a
book about YOU?

Would you
venture above

or below

or beyond—
with help from
a broomstick?

Or maybe
a wand?

Would you skip across
stars or a planet
or two?

Would you go it alone
or invite a whole crew?

Adventure
is waiting.

So much you can do

in this wonderful,
wander-filled
book about YOU.

Would you rescue
a king
or a queen
or a dog?

Would you capture a castle?
Sip tea with a frog?

Would you ride
on a dinosaur?

Romp with emus?

Would you dance with a yak
while you both play kazoos?

Would you cure polar bears of the polar bear blues—
The polar bear blues?
The polar bear blues!

Well, then!
Cure walruses too!

You don't have to choose!

You might create something
that changes a mind—

or makes a heart stir.
You might simply
be kind.

You might give a big speech.
Or defend something small.

You might open a window.

Or tear down
a wall.

And when trouble comes,
you might bravely stand tall.

You might muster your courage . . .
to rise from a fall.

Would you march slow and steady?
Or sprint from the start?

Would you follow the crowd?
Or lead from your heart?

The choices are endless.
The obstacles few.

So many chapters
beginning to brew.
Imagine the endless
good you might do,

in a heartwarming,
heart-building

book about YOU.

You might
read a book!

You might
write a book!

A powerful, page-turning,
book about you!

A book about you
in a book about
YOU?

Amazing!

Astonishing!

Astounding!

Absorbing!

Absolutely,
undeniably,
unmistakably ...
awe-inspiring—

times
two!!!

PHEW!

If your life were a book
with pictures and pages,
what would you do
to be read through the ages?

Stop.

Dream.

Think it through.

What would
you do in a book
about YOU?

The End . . . or, rather—
the Beginning!